Bear's Adventure

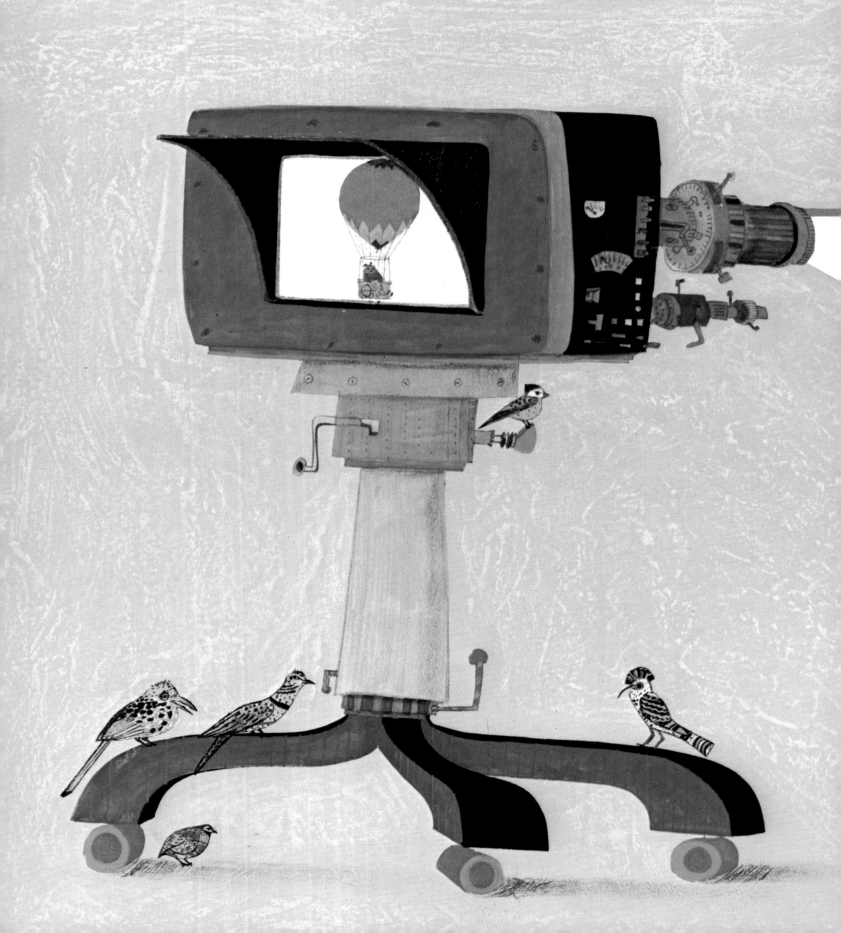

Bear's Adventure

BRIAN WILDSMITH

PANTHEON BOOKS

One fine morning, a brightly colored balloon carrying two men drifted slowly toward the mountains. "I'm hungry," said one man to the other. "Let's go down and have something to eat."

When they had landed, the two men walked off to look for a place to have their picnic.

While they were gone, a brown bear came up to the balloon. "I've never seen a den like this," he thought. "It looks like a good place to have a nap."

Bear climbed into the basket and found it so comfortable that he soon fell fast asleep.

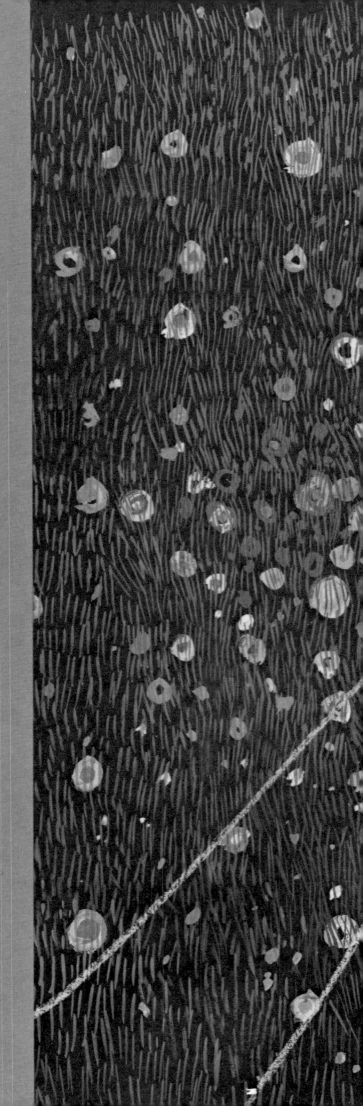

When Bear woke up, he was amazed to find that he was floating over what he thought was a strange forest of tall trees.

While Bear was trying to understand why these trees had no leaves, a bird, not looking where he was going, collided with the balloon. His beak punctured it, and the balloon lost air. Slowly it floated to the ground.

It landed in front of a costume parade that was just about to start. "How exciting!" said a man in the crowd. "What an original way to start the parade—dropping from the sky in a balloon. And what a magnificent costume! It looks so natural."

Bear was so alarmed by all the noise and excitement that he set off down the street. The crowd marched behind him, trumpets blaring.

Bear hadn't gone very far before a young man rushed up to him. "That was a marvelous entrance," said the man. "And what a great costume!"

"I'm a TV news reporter," he went on. "I'd like to interview you. Come along to the studio with me." And he pushed Bear into a taxi.

When they got to the studio, the reporter lit his pipe and offered Bear a seat. "What's your name?" he asked.

"Grr," replied Bear.

"Well, Mr. Grr," said the man, "where did you get your wonderful costume?"

Bear turned his head from side to side to look at the flashing lights around him. The reporter thought Bear was shaking his head. "Ah! I suppose you want to keep that a secret," he said, relighting his pipe.

Bear was hungry. He wanted to try some of whatever the reporter was eating. He grabbed the pipe from the man's mouth and put it into his own. Everyone started to laugh. This startled Bear, and he dropped the pipe and ran out of the studio as fast as he could.

Outside, a motorcyclist drove up to him. "That was a very funny act," he said to Bear. "I was watching you here on my portable television set. If there's anywhere you'd like to go, just tell me and I'll take you." And he revved up his engine.

"Grr grr grum," replied the bear as he climbed onto the motorcycle.

The motorcyclist thought Bear said "the sports stadium," so off he roared with Bear clinging on behind.

They got to the stadium just as a race was about to start.

"Bang!" went the starter's pistol, and away went the runners. Frightened by the noise, Bear jumped off the motorcycle and started to run. He moved so quickly that he soon overtook the racers. He ran faster and faster and crossed the finish line. Then he kept on running toward the exit while the crowd cheered and applauded.

"Isn't that the man who came down in a balloon to start the parade?" asked one of the judges.

"Yes," said the mayor, "and he's not only funny—he can run faster than our best athletes."

Alarmed by the roars of the crowd, Bear ran out of the stadium before the mayor could present him with the winner's medal.

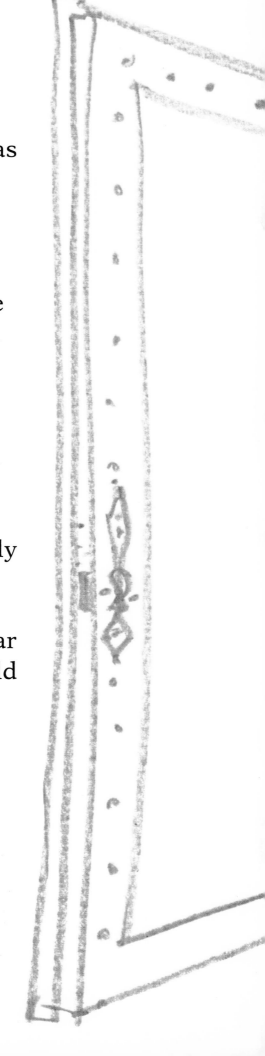

Outside the stadium, Bear almost bumped into a strange-looking bird with five wings. "Hop aboard," shouted a man inside the bird. "I'm going to a rock concert."

"What a strange and noisy bird," thought Bear as they rose into the sky.

The music at the concert was so loud that no one heard the helicopter land.

Bear was delighted with the music. So he climbed onto the stage and began to dance. The audience was thrilled by his performance and cheered and clapped and danced

along with him. When the music stopped, a crowd of people rushed toward Bear.

"That's the man who was so funny on TV," said one. "Yes," said another. "He also won the race at the stadium. And he's a great dancer too!"

Bear was terrified by all of the commotion and ran from the stage.

"We know how you feel," called a fireman from a fire truck that was parked nearby. "This crowd is very excited, but we'll get you out of their way. Climb onto the ladder and we'll hoist you into the air."

Bear thought it was a tree and started climbing.

The ladder rose into the sky as Bear climbed to the top.
Just then a balloon carrying two men came floating by.
"Look! Isn't that the man we saw on television earlier today?"
said one balloonist to the other. "He seems to be having
some trouble with his fans. I think we should help him."
Steering the balloon toward the top of the ladder, the two
men helped Bear climb into the basket.

Exhausted by the day's events, Bear immediately fell asleep.

The balloon traveled on until it was near the mountains. "I think it's time we had another bite to eat," said one of the balloonists. "Let's go down."

When they landed, the men tied their balloon to a large rock. Then they walked over to a nearby stream and spread out their picnic.

While they were gone, Bear woke up.

"How strange," he thought as he looked around.
And dazed and bewildered, he waddled away.

THE END

Library of Congréss Cataloging in Publication Data   Wildsmith, Brian. Bear's adventure.
Summary: Bear appears on television, wins a race, and dances at a pop concert—all
of which leave him slightly bewildered and quite exhausted.
[1. Bears—Fiction]   I. Title.   PZ7.W64 7Be   1981   [E]   81-18814
ISBN 0-394-85295-8   ISBN 0-394-95295-2 (lib. bdg.)   AACR2